PUZZLE ADVENTURE STORIES

THE HAUNTED HOTEL

SOLVE ITS MYSTERIES!

WINDMILL BOOKS

Lisa Regan

Published in 2019 by **Windmill Books**, an imprint of Rosen Publishing
29 East 21st Street, New York, NY 10010

Written by Lisa Regan
Illustrated by Moreno Chiacchiera
Designed by Paul Oakley, with Emma Randall
Edited by Frances Evans, with Julia Adams

Cataloging-in-Publication Data

Names: Regan, Lisa.
Title: The haunted hotel / Lisa Regan.
Description: New York : Windmill Books, 2019. | Series: Puzzle adventure stories
Identifiers: LCCN ISBN 9781508195412 (pbk.) | ISBN 9781508196280 (library bound) | ISBN 9781508195429 (6 pack)
Subjects: LCSH: Hotels--Juvenile fiction. | Haunted places--Juvenile fiction. | Puzzles--Juvenile fiction.
Classification: LCC PZ7.R443 Ha 2019 | DDC [E]--dc2

Manufactured in the United States of America

CPSIA Compliance Information: Batch #BS18WM: For Further Information contact Rosen Publishing, New York, New York at 1-800-237-9932

THE ADVENTURE BEGINS...

Ruby, her best friend, Ned, and her dog, Mungo, are excited. They are going to meet Ruby's Great Aunt Hilda! They don't know her yet, but she has sent the gang on many an exciting adventure. Hilda's throwing a big party on Halloween, and wants the kids and Mungo to come along. But, as usual, her message to them is far from straightforward. Make sure you have a pen and a piece of paper handy, so you can help solve any puzzles! You can find the answers starting on page 28.

4

Destination unknown

Ruby has asked Ned to come to her house right away. Great Aunt Hilda's throwing a party on Halloween and they're invited! But first they need to figure out which hotel she's staying at, when she'll be there, and what they need to bring. Use the code key that Hilda has sent to help them! Write down the solution on your piece of paper.

Code key

A = ☾ B = ✝ C = ✄ D = ✳ E = ❋
F = ✺ G = ✏ H = ✶ I = ✴ J = ✳
K = ✳ L = ❈ M = ✳ N = ☆ O = ★
P = ✬ Q = ✚ R = ✰ S = ✩ T = ✪
U = ☆ V = ★ W = ✧ X = ✦ Y = ✢
Z = ♣ ! = ♧ ? = ✛ & = ✡

Can I come, too?!

Dear Ruby and Ned,
Come to ✶✰✪✳✳✳ ☾✳✪★☾✰✳☆★☾
in the Spooky Mountains for my party! I will be
there from ✳✶✳✳✳☾✚♧ ✪☆✰ ✰☆☆✳✳☾✚♧.
✄✰☆✪☆✳✳✶✰☆ are essential! A taxi will
pick you up this evening.
Love,
Great Aunt Hilda

Switchback

The taxi arrives and they set off into the mountains. "Hmm," says their driver, checking the fuel gauge. "I'm running a bit low. We're going to have to take the quickest route, guys." Add up the numbers to figure out whether the red or the blue route uses the least amount of fuel.

Tread carefully

The driver pulls to a halt at a rickety bridge and points them in the direction of the hotel. The friends each have a different idea about how to get across the bridge. Which strategy will get them safely across? They must not step on any of the broken slats!

Ned: Jump three slats forward and then jump one back.

Ruby: Jump three slats forward each time.

Mungo: Jump two slats forward each time.

The fog

By the time they cross the bridge, it's getting dark, but they can just about see the hotel. The taxi driver gave them some clues on how to get to the entrance. Can you figure out which doorway they should go through?

CLUES:
1. It is beneath a lit window.
2. It is up some steps.
3. It is not the door in the middle.
4. It has a lit window to its right.

Err... this place looks a little spooky!

The cold reception

Although it's early evening, the place seems deserted. They ring the bell for service. An old man appears. When they ask for Great Aunt Hilda, he looks puzzled. "I haven't seen her since she first checked in. But it looks like she's taken her key." Can you spot which room Hilda is staying in?

Can you see who else is staying in the hotel?

Deserted

They collect the letter in Hilda's postbox and run to her room. The door is slightly open so they peer inside. Brr! It's freezing! But there's no sign of Great Aunt Hilda. Look for five clues that suggest she hasn't been in her room for some time.

Hot on the trail

Ruby leans out of the window. She can see a spooky graveyard and a maze on the hotel's grounds down below. "Let's check outside," she suggests. "Wait!" says Ned. "Have a look at this." He has opened the envelope from Hilda's postbox. It contains an old photo and a letter cut into pieces. Can you figure out what it says? Write down the answer on your piece of paper.

this is the

Remember

days, Hilda?

one of my evil plots!

last time

you thwart

Not anymore.

old

the good

Yours sincerely, P. Schnurrbart

Help!

Suddenly, the lights go out! Ned and Ruby head for the janitor's room. "Someone" has tampered with the electricity and plunged the hotel into darkness. Help them figure out how to turn the lights back on.

CLUE:
Look at the four sketches under the fuse box. Which one matches it?

Haunted!

The children head back to reception area where they are confronted by... a ghost? And a mummy in bandages, and a vampire! Yikes! Could these monsters be in cahoots with Dr. Schnurrbart? Ned and Ruby dive for cover. Can you spot where they've hidden?

I hope there's cake!

Strangely, Mungo doesn't seem afraid. He trots up to the mummy, sniffs deeply, and starts to lick him. What do you think is going on here?

Hide-and-seek

The kids emerge from their hiding places and head outside. Mungo barks excitedly. "Look! I think this is from Hilda's dress..." says Ruby. "Erm, do you feel like we're being watched?" stammers Ned. The garden is full of spooky statues, but some of them don't look quite right. Could they be Dr. Schnurrbart's henchmen in disguise?

CLUE:
The shadows that match are statues. The ones that don't should be avoided!

A   B   C   D   E   F

Crazy paving

The kids sneak past the monsters and follow Hilda's trail to a crumbling patio. There's a note lying on the grass with instructions on how to get across. Use the clues to trace a path with your finger and help the gang to get across.

The patio is ALARMED!!! You need to step on the correct stones to get to the gate undetected. Don't tread on the mossy stones. Only step on the stones that are multiples of three. When you get to the gate, head north!

On the right track

"Great Aunt Hilda definitely came this way," whispers Ruby. How can she tell?

CLUE:
Can you spot one of Hilda's gold earrings hidden in the picture? Look back to her photo on page 10 if you need to.

Which way now?

"We need to get to the northern corner of the graveyard," Ned reminds them. But which way is north? Find the weathervane that points to the directions in the correct order.

Captured!

As they reach the northern corner, Ned gives a shout and Mungo barks loudly. Ruby flashes her light in their direction, just in time to see them being dragged away. It was a trap! She runs after them, through a gap in the hedge... and finds herself in the maze! Can you help her get to the other side, avoiding Dr. Schnurrbart's costumed stooges? Trace a safe path with your finger.

The right moves

Once she's out of the maze, Ruby follows the sound of Mungo barking to a door in the basement of the hotel. "Ned!" she cries as she enters the room. She needs to figure out where to push the lever to open the cage. There's a scrap of paper with a puzzle on it pinned to the wall. Can you find the correct number by solving it on a piece of paper?

Days in a week = ?

−

Legs of a frog = ?

×

Number of fangs that a vampire has = ?

÷

Sides of a triangle = ?

total = ?

Schnurrbart's revenge

"A mummy grabbed me and Mungo!" Ned exclaims, as he climbs out of the cage. "But I think it was Dr. Schnurrbart in disguise. He said he's holding Hilda prisoner, here in the hotel. And then he gave me this..." They study the scrap of paper in Ned's hand. "I see a message!" gasps Ruby. Can you figure out what it says, too? Use your pen and paper to write down the message.

Which way now?

The children head for the door, and see a fire notice with a map of the hotel. Can you figure out which room they are in, and where they need to go to rescue Great Aunt Hilda, using the clues below?

CLUES:
1. Look back to page 18 to figure out which room the kids are in.
2. Dr. Schnurrbart's note mentioned dancing...

Memory test

They commit the route to memory and head off. But Dr. Schnurrbart has made plans to stop them. The door at the foot of the stairs is locked, and this time his message is clear enough. Can you think of a number the kids could try to open the safe?

HA HA!
Not so fast, kiddies! I've locked the key in the safe!

CLUE:
Think fast! Great Aunt Hilda is in a very GRAVE situation... (Look back to page 16 for your clue!)

Foiled again!

They got it! Ruby grabs a bunch of keys from inside the safe, they rush through the open door, and head upstairs. They hurtle down the corridor toward a pair of ornate doors and... gah! They are locked, too! Find a set of two matching keys to let them in, quickly!

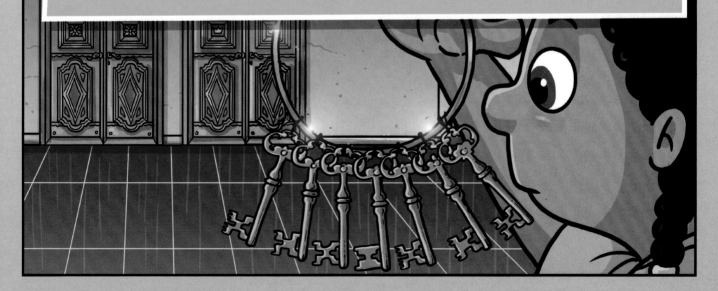

Mr. Bad Guy

They burst through the doors, skid to a halt, and assess the situation. They've found Hilda, but she is surrounded by mummies! "Good work, kids," says Hilda, with a smile. "But watch out! One of these mummies is Dr. Schnurrbart!" Can you help Ruby and Ned spot one mummy who is ever so slightly different from the rest?

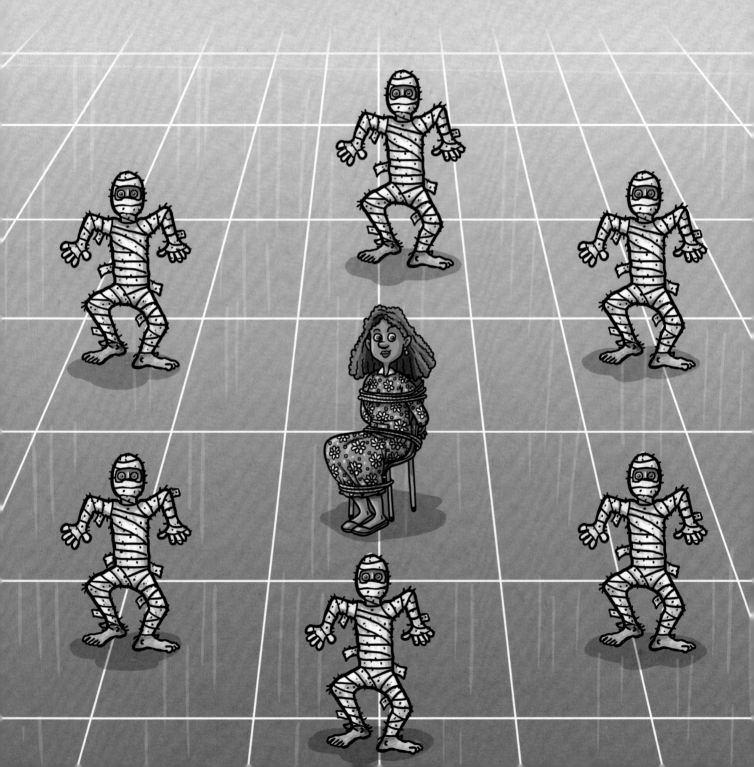

Mummy attack

"Ruby, Ned," shouts Hilda, "there are laser beams around the walls. Turn three pairs on so the mummies can't get to me!" The kids have switched on one pair. Which other two pairs of lasers will protect Hilda? Make sure you don't hit anyone! You can use a ruler to figure out where each laser beam will travel. Write down your answers on your piece of paper.

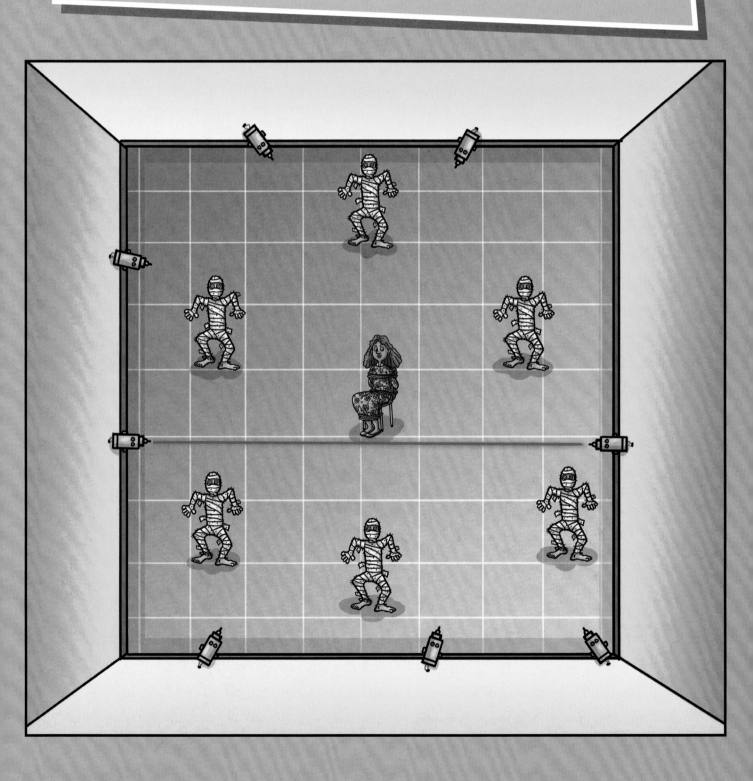

On his tail

Dr. Schnurrbart realizes the game's up and makes a run for it. The kids quickly turn off the lasers, untie Great Aunt Hilda, and chase after him. He's been walking around barefoot all night in the mummy costume and is leaving behind muddy footprints. Which set should they follow?

Back in disguise

They follow Dr. Schnurrbart's prints and find themselves in a cloakroom, full of Halloween costumes. He's changed his costume to try to shake them off! Which outfit has he stolen?

Vampire
Witch
Roman soldier
Werewolf
Princess
Ogre
Clown
Skeleton

Cornered!

Once they figure out he is dressed as a werewolf, the kids manage to track down Dr. Schnurrbart pretty quickly. He knows he's been cornered and dashes back into the hotel. "We've got him now, kids!" says Hilda. Spot the difference between the before and after photos on the children's phones to figure out which room Dr. Schnurrbart is hiding in.

Party time

They call the police, who march Dr. Schnurrbart away in handcuffs. Great Aunt Hilda claps her hands and smiles. "Well, that's settled. Now let's party! A quick costume change, children, and I'll see you back in the ballroom for some Halloween FUN!" If you are familiar with some of the gang's previous adventures, you may be able to spot some old friends at the party! How many can you see?

The party is one of the best the children have been to. But then, everything involving Great Aunt Hilda is exciting... even though it can be a little hair-raising sometimes! They can't wait to find out where Hilda will take them next.

Answers

Page 4 Hilda is staying at Hotel Altavista. She will be there from Friday to Sunday. Ned and Ruby must bring their costumes!

Page 5 The red route is the fastest.

Page 6 Ruby's strategy will get them across safely: jump three slats forward each time.

Page 7

Page 8 Hilda is staying in room 21. Dr. Schnurrbart is staying in room 26!

Page 9 1. The window is wide open and it's raining outside.
2. There is an unopened package by the door.
3. Hilda hasn't touched her breakfast and it's now the evening.
4. The calendar hasn't been changed.
5. The flowers in the vase have wilted.

Page 10 This is what Dr. Schnurrbart's message says:

Remember the good old days, Hilda? Not anymore. This is the last time you thwart one of my evil plots! Yours sincerely, P. Schnurrbart.

Page 11 D matches the fuse box.

Page 12 Ruby is hiding behind the knight on the left. Ned is hiding behind the curtain on the right. Mungo isn't afraid of the monsters because he can smell that they are just friendly partygoers!

Page 13 A and C are statues. B, D, E, and F could be Dr. Schnurrbart's stooges.

Page 14

Page 15 On the right track:

Which way now?:

Page 16 All of the people died when they were 63 years old.

Page 17

Page 18 Ruby needs to pull it to number 2 (7 − 4 = 3; 3 x 2 = 6; 6 ÷ 3 = 2).

Page 19 Read each line vertically: HILDA HAS LED ME A MERRY DANCE BUT NOW SHE WILL DANCE TO MY TUNE.

Page 20 The gang are in the laundry room in the basement. They need to get to the ballroom upstairs.

Page 21 Memory test: 63 will unlock the safe.

Foiled again:

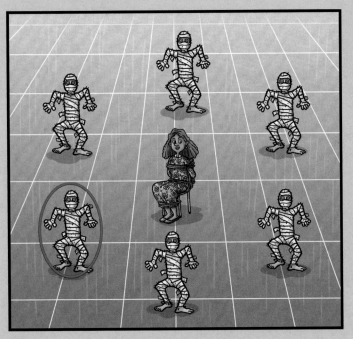

Page 22 Dr. Schnurrbart has a piece of bandage on his left elbow and brown eyes.

Page 23

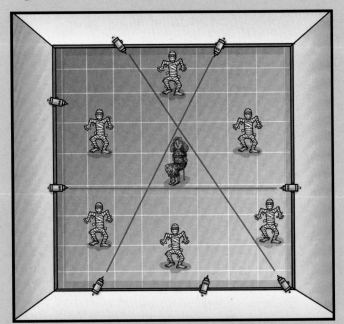

Page 24

Page 25 the werewolf outfit is missing.

Vampire
Witch
Roman soldier
Werewolf
Princess
Ogre
Clown
Skeleton

Page 27 Cousin Nico, Bob the Sailor, the talisman owner, Uncle Alf, and Jules.

Page 26

Glossary

fuse box A box that contains the fuses for all the electrical circuits in a building.

henchman Someone who is devoted to serve one particular person.

in cahoots To conspire together against someone.

ornate Highly decorated.

thwarted When someone has been stopped from doing something.

weathervane A pointer that moves with the wind and shows its direction.

Further Information

Books:

Dolby, Karen. *Ghost in the Mirror.* London, UK: Usborne, 2008.

Miller, D. L. *Bigfoot Visits the Big Cities of the World.* Happy Fox Books, 2018.

Websites

For web resources related
to the subject of this book, go to:
www.windmillbooks.com/weblinks
and select this book's title.

Index